Sunflower Island

BY CAROL GREENE

PICTURES BY LEONARD JENKINS

HARPERCOLLINS*PUBLISHERS*

The art in this book was created using acrylics,
spray paint, and pastels on acid-free museum paper.

Sunflower Island
Text copyright © 1999 by Carol Greene
Illustrations copyright © 1999 by Leonard Jenkins
Printed in the U.S.A. All rights reserved.
http://www.harperchildrens.com

Library of Congress Cataloging-in-Publication Data
Greene, Carol.
  Sunflower Island / by Carol Greene ; pictures by Leonard Jenkins.
      p.   cm.
  Summary: A young girl sees a sidewheeler run aground and over many years
describes how the river makes the remains of the wreck into an island and then washes
it away again. Based on a true story.
  ISBN 0-06-027326-7. — ISBN 0-06-027327-5 (lib. bdg.)
  [1. Shipwrecks—Fiction.   2. Rivers—Fiction.]   I. Jenkins, Leonard, ill.   II. Title.
PZ7.G82845Sl   1999   97-10703
[Fic]—dc21   CIP
                                                                                      AC

601697378

Typography by Al Cetta
1 2 3 4 5 6 7 8 9 10
❖
First Edition

For Peggy Mann
—C.G.

For Etta Taylor
—L.J.

Once there was a river,
a broad, blue river,
that ran swift and strong
to the sea.

Many boats traveled that river—
fine boats, humble boats,
and boats in between—
taking goods and passengers
upstream and down.

The *Sunflower* was one of the
in-between boats,
a side-wheeler who'd seen better days.
But though she was old and noisy,
she still could do her job
and she wore a bright new coat of paint.

One cold February night, the *Sunflower* steamed down the river, carrying flour, pigs, and a few passengers. Her owners, the Barclay brothers, were on board, too. Tom was the captain and Joe was the pilot.

Now, those two brothers never could get along. So when they came to a bend in the river with a shoal, a shallow place, in the middle, Tom said, "Let's go to the west. It's safer."

But Joe said, "No. Let's go to the east. It's faster."

On a boat, the pilot is always right, even when he's wrong. So the *Sunflower* swung to the east of the shoal, and that was her undoing.

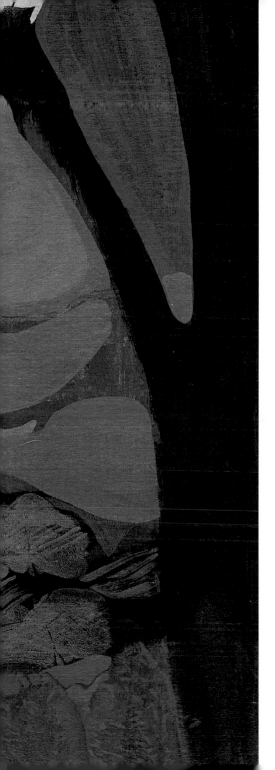

As the pale winter sun
began to stain the sky,
a snag, an underwater tree,
reached up from the river bottom
and tore a hole in the *Sunflower*'s belly.
In rushed the river to pull her down,
but other snags caught her
and held her fast.

There perched the *Sunflower*
like a big, bright bird,
half in and half out of the water.
And the river ran around her,
swift and strong to the sea.

No one aboard was hurt, and no one was afraid since the shore was near. But Joe mumbled excuses, and Tom said terrible things as they blew their whistle for help.

On the shore, a small girl named Polly watched from her bedroom window. She saw the *Sunflower* strike the snag and heard the whistle blow.

She saw her father run out to his rowboat. He rescued all the people, and together they rescued the pigs and the flour. Then Polly's mother served everyone breakfast.

But no one could do anything for the *Sunflower*. There she sat, and folks came from miles around to strip her of everything they could carry away. Polly's family got her deck railing and set it up as a fence around their house.

"Well, child," said Polly's mother as she tucked Polly into bed and kissed her good night, "I guess you'll always remember this day."

"Yes, Mama," said Polly. "I surely will."

Years passed,
and the river bottom rose.
It wrapped itself around the *Sunflower*
and held her tight.
At the same time,
the river nudged sand and silt
from the shoal.
It pushed them toward the boat,
piling some here,
spreading some there,
until her decks and cabins were covered.

Then the river brought gifts
to the *Sunflower*—
seeds, driftwood,
and tiny floating islands.
The tiny islands clung to the boat,
and the driftwood rotted into soil.
The seeds struck roots and sprouted
into lacy, green trees—
willows and cottonwoods.
Birds sang in their branches,
and animals rested in their shade.

"Look, child," said Polly to her own small daughter as they planted flowers along the fence. "That's Sunflower Island. I remember the day the old *Sunflower* sank."

She sat down on the ground, pulled her daughter into her lap, and told her the story as the river ran by, swift and strong to the sea.

More years passed,
and people began to use
the island as a pleasure place.
They dove from its banks
and had picnics under its trees.
They fished or sometimes just sat
and watched the river run by.

"Come, child," said Polly to her grand-daughter. "I'll take you to Sunflower Island. You know, I remember the day the old *Sunflower* sank."

She packed up a lunch and some fishing poles, and they rowed across to the island. Then Polly told her granddaughter the story as the river ran by, swift and strong to the sea.

Still more years passed,
and the river began to nibble
at the sand and silt of the island.
Tree roots loosened,
and the willows and cottonwoods trembled
whenever the wind blew.

The tiny islands floated away,
the birds and animals fled,
and still the river nibbled.
It pushed the sand and silt
until the trees tumbled down
and floated away too.

Then only the bones of the *Sunflower*
remained, bleak and bare above the water,
like the skeleton of a big bird.

"See, child?" said Polly to her great-granddaughter as they picked wildflowers along the fence. "That used to be Sunflower Island. Why, I remember the day the old *Sunflower* sank."

She leaned against the fence and her great-granddaughter leaned against her and Polly told the story once again as the river ran by, swift and strong to the sea.

For a long time,
the *Sunflower*'s bleached old bones
waited, helpless above the water.
Then one rainy spring,
the river gathered itself
into a great flood.

It rushed and roared,
swifter and stronger than ever,
and when it reached the *Sunflower*,
it lifted her up
and carried her away to the sea.

"Oh, look, everyone!" cried Polly from her front porch, and her family, who'd come to visit, hurried out to her. "It's all gone. There's only the river left now. And I still remember the day the old *Sunflower* sank. Have I ever told you that story?"

"Tell us again," said her family.

So they went back inside, and Polly sat down in her comfortable chair. Then she told her family the story of Sunflower Island one more time as the river ran by, swift and strong to the sea.

AUTHOR'S NOTE

Sunflower Island is based on a true story, the story of the *Juno**, a side-wheeler that traveled the Wabash River and met her fate near New Harmony, Indiana, in 1865. I have changed some details and added others, but the essence of the story remains the same and says something timeless about time and rivers and people.

—C. G.

*See "The Wabash," by William E. Wilson, in *The Rivers of America*, edited by Stephen Vincent Benét and Carl Carmer (New York and Toronto: Farrar & Rinehart, Inc., 1940).

E FICT Gre
Greene, Carol.
Sunflower Island /

$14.95 04/01/99 AGE-9873